AF347323

BETWEEN LOVE AND WAR

Chevick Giraldo

EDICIONES RUBEO

For my brother Evelio who believed
in love and freedom of his town.

The traces of war are eyes that watch those who walk without me-
mory. The ashes of the people will be flames that will burn
in the hearts that love freedom.

When Aarón met Aní that morning, thousands of things passed through his thoughts, but he never thought that above the mandates of inexorable time the rose would continue with its buds open waiting for the gardener. Nor did he imagine that he would walk barefoot on a real world where the long wait would strangle his dreams, and the roads would turn to dirt and mud. For her part, she assumed that love was a song of mermaids in the sea, and that she was willing to become one of them to cultivate that man she had always dreamed of.

He was her first love, her first man, the first star that would light the dark path for her in those dreams where ghosts sometimes wanted to eat her memory to erase any vestige of happiness. She had what any woman wanted: a beautiful, smart, and most of all, a down-to-earth dreamer.

He dreamed of a world without wars and without hunger, a world where tomorrow would have no shadows preventing free thought; a world free of ties in the feet and in the soul, a world where the differences were respect for life, and where those same differences were the democratic feeling of a good coexistence.

When the two of them first looked into each other's eyes, they understood that they had shared dreams and that they would nurture those dreams until life provided them.

Many times they wrote poems on the same paper

that they pasted on street corners, they gave them away on buses and in bars with the idea that everyone knew how much they loved each other.

It was easy to find poems like these:

"We are not moons or suns, but we are the light of love to illuminate the quiet nights when the world sleeps.

We are songs of love, prayer of a song of winds and guitars that travel beyond the sun.

We are the rails of the train that does not stop at the station; we are dreaming of white birds being moons to sleep there until the war is over, until the rifles are silenced.

We are the bow of an arrow that travels with the wind where there is no love to feed dreams to those who do not dream, those who do not laugh, those who do not sleep".

Someone read in some murals twenty-one years later: "We have walked in a world full of adversity, but we have managed to pass the flames that burn the feet and make the soul sick.

We have built bridges over troubled waters so as not to drown the dreams of love, the dreams of life.

We have set traps for the ghosts of bad dreams to reach the other side of the sea where there are moons and suns, where there are singers who sing of love.

On this mural we leave what we wanted to be: a reminder of love, a possibility of living in the eyes that read us when we both die at the right time ".

The night before, he had told her that the army was raiding house to house recruiting men for war and that he was afraid they would line him up.

Do you realize? The joy of having you next to me would no longer creep onto the roof, because maybe you will die on the battlefield; in war everything is possible except life.

"Yes", Aaron said looking out the window as his little Aaron played in the courtyard of the house at war. He also told her that night, that the war brought back bad memories because in it he had lost his father, and two of his younger brothers were missing.

Aaron shed a tear and then another, and behind it came a feeling that cornered him in his own memories without being able to avoid them. His father had been enlisted in the troops of General Macarais, and there he lost his life one day when the guerrillas ambushed them. The soldiers had walked all day and as night fell they came to a forest where they laid out their hammocks. It was a group against guerrillas made up of seventeen men, of whom he was the oldest of all.

Why was it there? The country was at war and General Macarais needed men on the battlefront, so three months after receiving a light military training he was sent to the battlefront under the command of Lieutenant Leguis, a man who, due to his implacable character, the entire regiment feared him.

She would have liked to hug her Sioux mother, but from the armored truck she could barely shout that she loved us, that she carried us in her heart no matter how strong the winds were.

Each one hanged up their hammocks and entrusted themselves to the god of war. No more than three hours had passed when the sky was filled with sparklers and the bomb cylinders echoed over the humanity of the soldiers.

From the hill the insurgents continued dropping bombs and a closed circle of mortar rounds and fifty point shots were decimating the soldiers'morale. The subversives began a sweep across the length and breadth of the camp, and there, the few survivors who remained, fell one by one. The last to die was my father, he managed to cross the forest and reach the river where he found some of his companions with their bodies mutilated by the bombs. Some of them closed their eyes as if wanting to close the way to death; He carried others in his prayers hoping that their sins, if they had them, would be lighter when it came to reaching the path of the eternal silences of death. At the edge of a ravine was the body of Leguis with its eyes open looking up at the sky and its chest full of blood; Now he saw him helpless, he didn't have a frown and his mouth full of foam yelling at them not to be screwed, to be boars like their parents, to defend the fucking country that had given birth to them, not to be fags or sons of bitch.

Behind the bushes he barricaded himself while he kept hearing dry shots as if they were entering the earth, or in some dying body scraping the last breath of life. Some birds flew from the forest with their wings burned, others fell very close to their lifeless feet. For a moment he imagined that he was dead and felt an icy cold creep into his bones. Now he knew that his life depended on good luck, perhaps on the old wooden Christ that his mother had given him on the day of his first communion, and that he did not take it off even to make love to his wife. He gave him a kiss, crossed himself and wrapped it around his neck as he said to himself: "What a shit is to die alone without anyone accompanying me in that journey of mystery that is death; I would like to die accompanied by cicadas and crickets with their melodious songs, and my mother's voice telling me that I am missing nothing from this world other than her love, her affection and her kindness ".

Where will I go after I'm dead? He thought as he took the last Habanero tobacco that his friend Félix had given him on a trip he made abroad ...

Could it be that after death there are only roads full of lights, and in each gothic light of peace that there is not here on earth?

Why do we have to die to find out?

He smoked his tobacco but this time he did not inhale it, the smoke made spirals of snails that spread through the forest until they completely disappeared from his sight.

Now he stopped his breath as if trying not to miss the shot, but something happened in his rifle that did not come out. He disengaged it several times but it was stuck in the chamber. The men were already very close and he no longer had time to run. He drew his pistol and waited for the right moment. In front of the squad came a man in a green beret dressed as a military man. There was something unique about this man in the way he walked that caught his attention. Yes, it was the commander who in a guerrilla takeover in Lower Patía had lost mobility of his left leg, and who had managed to take thirteen soldiers and an officer as prisoners of war, and exchanged for partisans imprisoned in the country's maximum security prisons.

Ros, the guerrilla commander, a man hardened by the battles fought, had attended an ideological school for several years, and trained militarily in life and death combats against the army and the paramilitaries.

Ros smelled the smell of tobacco and actually assumed that my father had no military strategy; he gave a signal to his men and in an enveloping circle when he mounted the pistol his body fell to the ground. The Christ remained intact, but his life was taken by Ros in the dialectic of war: if you do not kill you are killed, you live or die.

It was his son who brought him back from his memories when he said pointing his pneumatic pistol at him: Daddy, do we play war?

No, it is not good to play war son, because it feeds bad dreams and it eats the good ones, he replied.

And why is there war, daddy?

Some believe that it is the way to achieve peace, for others, it is a lifestyle.

I do not understand much of what you say, but I would like to sleep without fear rather than she eating my dreams as a child.

All children have the right to be children and to live as children and not as adults.

You are right my son, only that behind the good thoughts there are others who want to eat the good ones at any cost.

Like Amat's father.

What happened to Amat's dad?

Went to war

Yes?

Do you remember him?

Yes son.

The one who competed barefoot in the marathon last year to get the attention of children walking barefoot around the world.

What happened?

He did not return.

Amat told me crying that he had lost his life on the battlefront, that he wanted to be great to avenge his father's death.

And what did you say to him?

That I would do the same.

Why?

So bad dreams don't eat good ones.

It's not okay to think about that, because hatred brings more hatred and the circle never ends.

But then do we have to pass over the corpse of the people we love the most without spitting on the executioner?

Aaron turned his back on him so that he would not see tears in his eyes, but his son asked him:

Do you remember my grandfather's death?

Maybe if you had spit hate bullets at them you would have healed by now, he said.

Without giving him time to think and looking into his eyes, I answered:

And why don't we kill those who killed him? I accompany you, I hate them.

His father hugged him for a long time and with a broken voice said: "Because that's not how you get peace."

So you don't plan to avenge my grandfather's death?

Aarón embraced him again, took him in his arms and as if wanting to end this conversation he replied: "It would bring more pain to the pain, maybe I would lose my life and then you would avenge me, or those who I would kill would avenge their deaths, then the role of hatreds would not end, neither would the war".

Do you understand me, son?

Yes, Daddy, I understand you, only that my grandfather died without me knowing him.

So what will happen to this war where innocents die?

Let me read you a little story about the future of war.

Once upon a time there was a king who enslaved people, and every time he had dreams of peace he would invent a war and fight with his neighbors. Peace for him was a nuisance, because he said that the spiritual food for the body was war, that it was through it that lies the balance between life and death, between being born and dying. One day the neighbors revealed themselves and could not bear the king's tantrums, each one passed the word to the other, and soon the slaves and neighbors rose up and dethroned the king. The king did not resist because he thought at the time that it was a dream. It was on the third day that he was taken to the main square of the town and executed there. Before he cried, but he did not ask for forgiveness because he was convinced that in the afterlife he would be king of kings, perhaps an immortal king, who, from there would rule his people and his neighbors again for the eternity.

And where is the moral of the story?

That war has masters and peace is a white flag that they want to dye with blood even in the afterlife.

I don't want to be a king or a slave, I want to be what I want to be, he said without wanting to end the conversation.

What do you want to be a son?

"Free"

Since that day his son Aaron did not play war again, but he did not stop thinking of freedom as a means of being happy while living here on earth.

On any given day while they were sleeping, the army arrived, they did not knock on the door, they entered and took him out as if he were a criminal. Aní begged them not to take him away but the officer told him that if his mother lived he would also take it away, because the country needed people with bravery in their balls to defend the country from the clutches of communism.

The boy asked him what communism was, and the officer told him that it was a doctrine that wanted to make the rich slaves and the poor to become the masters of the rich. He did not understand what he said, but what he did notice was that the officer's eyes changed color, and that for a short time he was stroking the grip of his pistol as if not wanting to forget who he was.

Aaron for his part looked into his eyes with anger, and wanted to tell him that he did not want to die in the war and that this war did not belong to him, and why the sons of the rich did not go to the battle front to defend their wealth, and in return they who did not have it, had to die for them. He later did not understand why he did not tell him, perhaps because he hoped the lieutenant would remember that his father had died when he commanded the patrol, and that it was not fair also to leave his little Aaron an orphan.

The lieutenant did not give him time to hug them and tell them that he loved them and that they were the light of his life, because he immediately ordered to throw him like a lump of potato on the train, where hundreds of young people with their heads shaved ignored the fate that awaited them. .

Lieutenant, rest assured that if he dies, I will not

give birth to children again for war and my little Aaron will hate you for life just like me; this was yelled at by his wife before closing the door and crying like never before.

From that day on, his life changed; during the day he would lock himself in the room and at night he would go up to the terrace until the last star was hidden. Her son Aaron asked her the first time what she was looking for there and she told him in a plausible voice: the door of heaven to shelter me from the absence of your father and from this prolonged sadness that is eating my bones.

Aaron lasted thirteen days in the regiment and then embarked on the red zone where intense combat to the death was fought. The first day the lieutenant took a magazine and walked through each of the rows, while telling them that the one with the big balls and the black heart survived here; that here the fight was fighting and that there was no weakness in the butt, that the one with the loose pants should take two steps forward to shoot him. When he was reaching the last row, he stood in front of Aarón, looked him straight in the eyes without blinking for a second and spitting out part of the tobacco he was smoking, he said: Do you have loose pants?

If you have weak ones, he will be the first to shoot; I haven't killed anyone for three days; He told him that, pulling out the nickel-plated gun and pointing it directly at his head. Aaron felt hatred and wanted to spit in his face, maybe he wanted to be the first to kill. He had plenty of reasons when his father died and left him abandoned in the bush; since then he had not been able to resolve the conflict of the duel, nor to cry over his grave.

That night he thought of his little family and an occasional tear escaped his eyes. He remembered the words he said to his little son about hatreds, and the role that war unleashes when we carry out revenge. It is not good to play war because it feeds bad dreams and eats up the good ones.

But what was he doing there?

Wanting to change the face of pain for another pain?

Killing his own class brothers?

Had his father's death changed the face of the war?

What if I die, and other steps follow my son until he is involved in war too?

Many fragile thoughts crossed mountains and mountains until falling into a deep sleep where his little Aaron was on a white horse, in his hands he carried a white flag and on his head something that looked like a bright sun was lighting a path full of stones and mud. . On those stones there were forgotten dead and on the side of the road I heard screams that were lost with other screams embracing death, perhaps looking for the closest way to escape from life. He never dropped the flag even though part of it was burned, and some words that said "peace or death" were already stained with blood. He came to a river and side to side there were men posted with their rifles full of bullets, and with their eyes full of hate waiting to quench their thirst for death. A shot was heard and then another. The horse snorted and was lost in the water. The white flag began to float over the rough waters as Aaron traveled to the bottom of the lifeless river. The men continued firing until the flag disappeared by the time the first shots were fired in the camp.

He did not know when his dream was interrupted by reality when the first bombs fell and he saw his friend Lear fly through the air, and a rifle blast took the life of a second corporal named Garden. He crawled to a place where he thought he was safe and from there he started firing his AK-44. The insurgents yelled at them, telling them they were sons of bitch and to dig their own holes in the ground because their hours were counted. He looked in his head for a prayer from the Lord of Miracles but could not find it, his memory was distorted and his thoughts were diatribes between life and death, between a time that recounted his stay here on earth, and others that told him that It would have been better not to have been born in this fucking world to die for others who had no soul, nor dreamed of white butterflies in the sky, but of putting more anonymous dead in the mountains, or in a forgotten street in their country. Next to him was Lieutenant Leguis with his frown and sweaty body; he could immediately perceive his hatred and the desire to kill. He had been trained for that next to the green berets of which the results were the order of the day. Among the undergrowth about a hundred meters into the darkness he fired responding to a rifle flash, in the distance he heard a weak cry and then a groan that was lost with the death of the guerrilla. The lieutenant looked at Aaron and didn't stop feeling a joy that ran through his veins. He leaned a little closer and whispered in his ear: tonight I can sleep soundly but I would sleep better if I finish with everyone. There was a short silence that maybe everyone took advantage of to reload their equipment, also to continue advancing in their imaginary as each one would win the next advance. Each one knew that the slightest carelessness or mistake would cost them their lives, and that here it was not a matter of winning only a battle, but the war. The lieutenant had been at this for more than thirty years, but he also knew that before its birth the country was at war and that the rebels were as skilled in the art as he. Here there was no tiger fight with a tied donkey, here there were no flowers or romantic love affairs, here the fight was fighting. So with one more death in his almanac, he was filled with more courage, and ordered his men to block the river where the resistance could attack from the other flank. His men crawled through the darkness like lizards carrying out his orders, but upon arrival they were greeted with crossfire from all sides. Arel, a young man from the peasant stratum and neighbor of Aaron, was the first to fall. He heard him say: "They killed me, friend, they killed me." A bomb completely destroyed his chest and another burst of the rifle killed Morón, a soldier who since he was recruited knew that he was going to die because of his bad training. Aaron crawled looking forward to help his friend but that was when he realized that it was too late, he had a large tear in his chest and part of his right hand was gone.

The burned trees and the hot earth, the smell of gunpowder and death riding on the shoulders of each combatant, it was as if he lived in a world where being born was the least important, because coming out alive was a dream of leaf litter that sucked down the breath and life of each survivor .

Now it was the voice of a lieutenant that crossed the distances, Aarón thought it was a way to combat his own fears, or his own demons as well, demons with which he had always lived since he left the body of his father and his men abandoned in the battlefield.

Here we are, sons of bitch, he yelled and sometimes he shot like he wanted to kill his own shadow.

Surrender, you have no escape, surrender.

On the other side there was silence but then it was interrupted by an earth-shaking roar. Some bodies flew through the air, others lay breathless watching their souls escape from their bodies.

Are you there lieutenant?

Are you there?

It was Aaron's voice cornered between fear and courage, between a kind of feeling where you want to run away but also to face a clean body regardless of whether you die or live. He already looked through the dawn lights and could see his commander with eyes sparkling with hatred asking him to help him, not to be a son of a bitch, not to let him die in the middle of the bush and in the hands of his executioners.

Aaron for a moment wanted to leave him lying like he did with his father, but then he thought that for today he was fine.

When Aaron picked him up he realized that his left leg was broken and that he had lost two fingers of his left hand. The lieutenant spat out curses and simply told him to call for air reinforcement. Immediately, helicopters and artillery planes arrived, machine-gunning the area, killing some combatants, including the man in third command of the rebel group. This man was Luan, a rebel who had become great in the organization by organizing the seizure of an embassy where he managed to negotiate the release of some of his fellow prisoners in the jails of his country. Luan died after facing them, managing to shoot down a ship with its occupants. His teammates immediately closed the game and managed to capture the ship's occupants alive. They were the first prisoners of war from that fighting front; a victory that raised the spirits of some and put them on a tightrope.

The fighting lasted three days and three nights, until, without any agreement, each side silenced their rifles, and took refuge with their dead in the jungle until the third day.

The displacement was immediate. Hundreds of peasants left the combat area, some managed to remove their belongings, others with what they had on; those wounded and killed by the bombardment were transported on mules and in makeshift hammocks; the fears were great but it seemed that here each one was the owner of what he had: his own sufferings. The roads were mined and some lost their limbs in their escape, others were killed in the first moment of the explosions.

The press and radio spoke of hundreds of wounded and dead, including Ros the leader of the rebels. When Aní heard this, she did not stop thinking that her husband had also died. She locked himself in his room and turned off the lights as if wanting to deny reality to the outside world. She imagined it traveling to that dark world of hidden silences where there is no return. She screamed his name and cursed the lieutenant a thousand times and even prayed out loud that he would die with his mouth full of mud. That day she did not come out, nor at night, there she was sometimes bent over her own shadow wondering why him, but she did not find an answer. Then she screamed, then again, until she felt that she had released some of her bad energies. In the street she looked for the newspaper and there was said what she heard on the radio. She went to the church looking for the priest but he had thrown off his cassock and had gone to throw lead in the mountains. Some parishioners had left behind, because if the church leader was ready to offer his life for the revolution, why not they who were sinners. Among them was Sian, a man in his seventies who was convinced that priest Bous had the power to return lives, because he had taken him out of the clutches of death once they were going to bury him alive because they assumed he had woken up dead.

Aní visited hospitals and there she was able to see the magnitude of the war. Children, women and the elderly lying in the corridors with serious injuries waiting to be treated. Some were already dead, others stuck in their beliefs to have a better trip to the other world.

The lieutenant was there recovering from his wound and reading the town's tabloid newspaper; When he saw her with frightened eyes, he said: he is alive, he has his balls on well, he will soon replace me in command, the only thing he needs is to eat a living dog, so he loses the sensitivity of the little humanity he has left. Aní felt disgusted by him, and again in silence she wished that when he died he would not come out of hell for a thousand years. He read her thoughts and immediately told her: I'm going to live until I personally finish off those shitty communists.

Go with God, since I can't go with him. This he told her when she slammed the door shut, but also with a hatred that she could not hide for the rest of the week.

Sitting on the chair that led to the door where he had been pushed out and then thrown on the train, she thought again of the wonderful moments when she met him. He was dressed in white and in his left hand he held balloons that he released one by one. The balloons at half height were exploding while with his gaze fixed on her, he invited her to participate in that innocent and full of color show. Imaginaries flew and soon assumed they were inside a giant balloon that carried them where only they existed. On that trip, heaven and earth were promised and they swore that the dreams lived would cultivate them until the sun melted the earth, and that if there was still life left, then they would bet on other dreams to live in the eternity of time.

Soon his son Aaron was born surrounded by the chirping of the birds of the field and the magical noise that the wind makes when it hits the trees. They grew wheat there until one day the scroll looked out of their window, and they ran to the big city, leaving everything behind. Soon they entered the dark cordon of misery where they had to experience the inclement cold, hunger and abandonment. Gone are the shots, but this new experience filled them with another pain: the pain of displacement, helplessness and uprooting.

In those days he learned of his father's death. It was one of the hardest blows after her mother's death from terminal cancer. That day he cursed the war, and came to think that he should not have been born at that time for his dreams to be made of colors and not of blood. The lieutenant was at the symbolic funeral, it was the first day he met him, he wore his lapel full of stars and a handwritten speech written by his lieutenant.

As soon as he began to read the speech, Aaron approached the coffin and demanded him for the corpse of his father; the lieutenant had no words to answer him because he knew what happened that day; so he threw away the paper and then lowered his head. Aaron spat on the ground and then looked at him with eyes of rage while the assistants booed him, and told him that he would likewise go to die in abandonment and eaten by vultures in the jungle. The lieutenant ordered them to be repressed but the priest Bous shouted at him: no more deaths, lieutenant, that's enough.

Moons and suns have passed since the last time Aní saw him; in that long time she had armed imaginary worlds of love so that those same worlds would keep her feet on the ground. It had been a long time since the day he boarded the midnight train with his watery eyes and a white handkerchief waving it in his hand. The train, without caring, was taking her dreams, her joys, on the rails, also a piece of her life. At her side were women and men who were mourning the departure of their children; some were dressed in black to mourn a farewell without return. How she would have wanted him to have been born in another time , to not see him leave on the war train, without a doubt that somewhere in the world they would have met and would have reaped love under another sky, under other moons. But the country was at war and the children of the rich did not go there, she knew that.

But why him? Was it the fault that the lords of power had made the country shit, and others were in revolt against the established order?

Was it not easier to distribute the national wealth among the poor, and avoid the deaths and the ruins of that national wealth?

She knew that her country was not the exception

because there were not only rich nor poor; a third of the planet was rich and the rest was full of poor people like them. But her country had been at war since she could remember, and if she had survived, maybe it was by chance, or because some star in the sky was watching over her.

The civil war continued to claim innocent lives on both sides and the unarmed population. The pastures were burned and in the windows of the houses the gunpowder ate the dream of all its inhabitants. The trains arrived full of the dead with their ashen eyes staring at the sky, and others on mules from different places. Some could mourn their children, but others kept the doors of their houses open in the hope that they would appear.

War brings everything except life expectancy. This she thought while searching for a light feeling that would take her to another place in her dreams, but she had realized that it was only a feeling because in her dreams there were men who wanted to eat her insides.

How longer? She wondered back home.

She wanted to find an explanation of why war, why some had to die for others to live when she did not see it as the way for the sake of peace and the dreams of humanity, but the extermination of any sentiment no matter how laudable.

She settled into the armchair that faced the window and from there, she listened to the train slide its rails on the damp iron. She looked out the window and hundreds of other young people were embarked on the train of death, the train that did not bring back the living but those who died on the front lines. She remembered the moment of his departure, his sad gaze penetrating hers, and an anxiety eating her life. She wanted to scream, run, maybe go back to being a girl to reconnect with a different landscape from the one she was living in, and there build a nest where the bombs in the streets would not break the windows of the houses.

After that day came others full of drama, but she always hoped that the train of death would bring her husband back. Sometimes she slept in the train station with her son, other times alone with her eyes open waiting for her return. There, in a fetal position, she remembered his last words coming out of a pitcher where emptiness has no end. "My love, if this train has no return and the eagle's wings are clipped, look for me in the place where the silences are infinite, and where the moon and the sun sing to those who leave the earth."

She wept for a long time, and then she understood that between life and death there is a dark abyss that leads us to where we never return, because death weighs more than life itself.

One day the train arrived early, but no men came there singing their victories, it brought the remains of the men who came out beating white handkerchiefs in farewell. All ran with scared eyes with hope stuck between their bones waiting to see their beloved; some were recognized, others were masses of meat burned by the bombs. She wanted to cry, but she had no tears; she wanted to insult the warlords but the cold gaze of a general made her understand that it was not the time yet. She kept his words but vowed one day to spit in his face if he was among the dead.

That morning at the train station the general spoke

in the midst of the dead, but no one listened to him, she would have wanted to anticipate and spit in his face but she hoped that Aaron was not there with ashen eyes looking up at the sky.

The dead were not counted but they were mourned. Ani was relieved when she did not find Aaron, but she did not stop thinking that he was cold somewhere on the battlefield.

A girl jumped on the body of her young father, began to scream and ask why the war, and why did some have to die for others to live. No one answered her because maybe they too had the same unanswered questions. She looked at the general who was still talking about the values of the war, as if this was not responsible for the deaths.

"This is the beginning of a fight that corresponds to all of us, he continued, saying, each combatant who dies is the fertilizer and the encouragement for others to continue on the path. When the communists die on the earth the new grass will be born and on the roofs of their houses the bad dreams of losing freedom will no longer creep in".

General, do you have a mother, father or siblings?

Is this the country you want, the country of the dead?

Why do we innocents have to lay the dead?

This was said by pointing to those who were lying on the floor and looking him in the eyes, but the general did not answer her, maybe out of cowardice, maybe he did not know the pain, nor the mercy of those who suffer it.

What freedom is he talking about?

About the freedom to lock ourselves in our own

pain and to cover every crack of our dreams with more dead? Is that the freedom you want for our people?

The general stared at her with eyes of fire, he made his way through the dead and when he was three meters away he drew his weapon and pointed at her he said: "About the freedom to free the earth of communist seeds like you."

And what is being a communist, General?

The General spit on the ground and walked away with the answer biting his lip.

After the day of his departure Aní never closed the door of his house or of his heart, perhaps she waited for the spirit to enter and lie down slowly next to her and tell her how his death had been, and how many nights he had longed for her kisses and body. She looked at the photo on the wall and there, she silently told him that she loved him more than her own life, that he was her spiritual food, the honeycomb where the bee slept.

She took a pen and a paper and began to write with her heart: "For you I have built imaginary bridges to escape the cruel reality that I am living, on those bridges I see you running towards me with open arms, and with a bouquet of flowers to tell me that I am too your expression of life and the encouragement to continue living.

On those bridges there are also birds that fly through the skies, they have their feathers broken by the war, but you tell me that they will survive because they will be the messengers of peace when the confrontation ends. So I ask you if you survived it, and you tell me that you are mountain and land, and the song of the condor that was born to fly away.

I am afraid that when I wake up I will not see the sun in my window, and the condor will fly without feathers through the skies. Give me your hands in your dreams and lead me to create other imaginary bridges when they breaks under my feet. I am afraid of being alone in the midst of the dead and the town on fire. I burned the place where our son was born. He asks me about you every day and sometimes the words catch in my teeth, but I tell him that you are at war but will return soon.

And why in the war, mommy? He asked me, I told him that the world is unequal because of the rich and that they try to fix it with the death of the poor.

That's not right mommy, he told me; but if my father dies I will go to war and avenge his death.

Against whom son?

Against the general, or with those who go barefoot fighting the army?

He looked at me without understanding anything, but we both knew that the loss of one meant as much as the other.

I'm writing you this letter, but the postman is dead; the roads are smeared with blood; the bombs fall on the roofs of the houses; the bridges swim as if they were floating houses in the rivers, and the most terrible thing, the dead are left with their eyes full of dirt and mud in the city and the fields.

My love, it is twelve o'clock at night, I hear the bombs fall in the corners and swallow the sleep of the inhabitants, the children cry and the old people make caves in the earth trying to save themselves. The city is dark and the smell of dead gunpowder prevents us from breathing. I hope to finish writing before the candle stops lighting to tell you that in my heart I have an immense flame of love that warms my feet, and that I hope it lights yours where you are. We both know that this war does not belong to us but it is evident that we have been involved in it. I only hope to see you arrive with your eyes sparkling with joy despite the fact that you bring the hands smeared with blood from other brothers who have died in this fratricidal war.

Our son has grown up, but I am afraid of it because without a doubt they will send him to the battlefield, and it will no longer be one letter that I will write, but two that may not arrive. I have proposed to mothers not to give birth to more children until the war is history, and not an irreverent truth that burns our dreams. We have also built a mural to all those who died in combat, not only from the regular forces but from the insurgency because we consider that it is a brother people faced by the exclusive interests of the rulers.

Here in the middle of these four cold walls of the house I continue to cultivate the seed of love and hope; I keep flying on the wings of white butterflies until I break the fears that sometimes chain me in dark eddies, and take me to deep voids where there are ghosts of war that want to eat me with their large mouths full of fire.

I do not want the time to die, I want the time of war to stop and the rifles to be silenced in the name of peace, in the name of the children who are seeds of the future, in the name of the fallen who fight without knowing why.

My love, let me tell you that today a bird sat at my

window, its wings were broken and the color of gunpowder carried it on its body. He looked at me with the same look full of sadness that you said goodbye, and I could see that he had the brown color of your eyes. I had no need to guess his suffering because I immediately understood that he came from the world of war. Then I imagined that you were the bird that had survived the storm, and that now it came home to continue our dream, the dream of peace and love. I asked him if the war was over but his eyes said no, then I understood that the wait continued but that you were alive, maybe walking home.

Many moons and many suns have passed since you left and here I continue to cultivate the garden of waiting, but if ever the eternal silences have led you to the place where there is no return, I will continue to cultivate the seeds of life so that our love do not die because of the war.

Before saying goodbye, I want to tell you that our son has been dreaming of seeing you arrive in a paper boat for a year, on the boat there are doves of the colors of all the countries and you are the captain of the boat. Pigeons fly all over the city and in one of them you get home. In the house there are other white doves that are the insurgents and there, forgetting their hatred, they drink wine and eat bread. You bring bright eyes with joy and instead of a rifle you bring white roses for Aaron and me. There are also mothers, wives, girlfriends, brothers and children loaded with bouquets of flowers, embracing the living and asking for the dead. Some cry in silence, others shout for joy; There are also glances among the mourners looking for their executioners, but you tell them that there are neither winners nor losers because on the battle front they have laid down their arms, they have realized who is responsible for the war and who benefits.

Ros, the leader of the insurrection, remains at his side; He says that among the combatants they are going to control the destinies of the country and that they are going to expel all the tyrants from the country. My son applauds and in the main square the mob awaits them. There is no resistance and the people celebrate victory.

It is enough for me to tell you that among the scaffolding of time there is a bird that struggles to break the glass and be by your side, that since you got on the train of death I have done nothing but wait for you without any conditions, because you are the eyes that illuminate my road and my destination, you are the mountain that gives air to my lungs.

My love, without you there is no light, without you there is no life, you are the reason for my existence, forever ".

She did not finish sealing the letter when a bomb from the air ended up smashing the windows of her house. Shouts and lamentations could be heard in the street as the bombs continued to fall like hail on the streets and houses. The city was engulfed in black smoke as insurgents from the town's shore shot down planes and helicopters.

She began to move her eyes and realized that the roof of the house was not there, she looked around and there was little Aaron with his gaze lost in pain with glass embedded in his head. He let out a scream that was swallowed up by the noise of the planes and rifles firing. She took him in her arms and ran to the hospital; She asked for help but the people ran with their own dead. The hospital was left with a rubble wrapped in twisted iron and inside other dead people who swam in silence and oblivion.

She continued through the dusty streets in the midst of the dead looking for help but realized that there was no one to help. She sat on the corner of the street and it was when she realized that Aaron eyes had lost the brightness of life, and that his son had died. She kissed him, hugged him, and cried this moment as one of the bitterest of her life. She spat words against the warlords and wanted to tell the general that he was an ill-born son of a bitch, that when he died the ghosts of war would eat his soul so that he would never dream of rifles and grenades again. She looked at the sky as if wanting to find answers, but maybe the angels were also fleeing the events of the war.

Where is God?

She screamed on her knees but no one answered.

On the way back, she did not find her home, there were only ashes and the photo of her husband floating on them. She took it and kissed it, then placed it in her bosom as if wanting to listen to the beating of his sad heart.

His little Aaron was buried on the ashes and on those ashes she wrote: "Now that you have gone to heaven wrapped in the colors of the rainbow I have stayed in the land of fire; in the land of war.

Where would you sleep now? She took one last look at where for years she cultivated the dreams of her husband and her son, now she had nothing. She walked the streets but now did not care if a rifle shot or a bomb would end her life. It was like walking in a world that she did not want to know anything about, but that was there taking away the reason to live step by step.

Ros was born into a poor family, where the daily struggle was not to walk barefoot for hours to get to his school, but to get on his good feet through an anti-personnel mine. His three brothers had been enlisted in the war, and his parents had been assassinated by paramilitary gangs. When he was seven years old, his childhood was buried in dust and mud, in the ghosts that haunted him in the dark nights, in the dreams of men with big mouths that threatened to eat him alive. In one of those dreams someone entered; he settled down next to him and from there he took him to a river where all the inhabitants of his town floated. The men's eyes were open and covered in mud. Their hands were painted whitewash and on them signs that said goodbye to the earth and welcomed them to hell. Among the men was the village priest, he remembered him because he had mourned his father's death the day he was killed by paramilitary gangs in the service of the regime. He approached him and asked him in his ear if there was another hell outside of this one, but he did not answer, then, he looked at the man who accompanied him, but before he asked him he said: "the only way to know is to be dead and I am the one chosen to take you to the end point ". He opened his mouth and there was fire. The man followed him until he was lost among the dead floating in the river. When he woke up he felt the sensation that the man of fire was still following him; He looked for the priest but was told that he was floating on the river with his eyes open on his way to heaven. From that day on, he could not continue to differentiate between reality and dreams because both were direct paths to hell.

One day back at school he wondered if this was the country where his children would grow up and cultivate peace, love, wheat and respect for life. The answer was found when he heard screams that crossed the roads where he walked every morning; He peeked through the cracks of his house and there he saw his mother being raped by several men in front of his father. Her body was bathed in blood and bruises all over the body. His eyes widened, and he could see that she was missing a few fingers on her left hand and that her hair had been cut in parts. She was tied to a tree hand and foot and her body was supported by the men who raped her. The men laughed and told him that it was a war trophy, that war brought benefits like this, and that as long as they existed, these blessings would not cease to exist. His laments were dry now, and little by little they were lost until he heard only the moans of the men. The men withdrew and shot him point-blank in the head a meter away. Now he could see her well, she was missing part of her right foot and a river of blood came from her head that reached where his father was. Now he looked at his father, he had no eyes and also his limbs had been cut off in a cruel and brutal way. He heard him breathing hard after a sharp blow from one of them with the butt of a rifle. They told him to regret being a shitty communist and logistically supporting the guerrillas, but he did not respond. Then one of them took three steps forward, stuck the gun in his mouth and his skull was scattered on the tree.

Ros ran into the bush while the men shot and shouted at him, that he was also a communist seed and that their mission was to prevent those seeds from growing and bearing fruit so that the world would continue as it was in the hands of those who had the weapons, because whoever had the weapons had the power. He jumped streams and pipes; fell and got up; sometimes he thought that he was flying but also that his wings were burned by rifle flashes. He kept hearing gunshots, sometimes crashing into trees, other times hitting his body. When he thought he was free, a column of men surrounded him; now he was imprisoned and handed over to other men who took him to a camp where there were corpses thrown on the ground with coup de grace, others with their feet burned with signs of torture. He was tied to a tree where perhaps others had lost their lives. He looked among the dead and there was his father's best friend, a peasant who could not read or write, but accused by this criminal organization of writing the pamphlets alluding to the resistance. Also at his side was a woman and two children, it was his wife and his little family. He kept looking, and there were some of his neighbors, all oblivious to the armed conflict that the only sin was being born at this time and in the wrong place.

A boy of the same age approached. His eyes did not have the expression of a child, but of a man who might have walked over the corpse of his mother without caring about anything. He had a rifle that came down to the ground, and he raised it and pointed it at him. He shot it but hit the post. He pointed again but a man behind him shouted: Leave it to me, I do not miss. The man had a white pistol and a necklace full of bullets on his chest. He started to fill the cartridge and then blew it when he mounted it.

The boy with the big rifle told him to please leave it to him, that the next shot would not miss, the man reluctantly accentuated by spitting in Ros's face. The boy unlocked the rifle; He looked happy, he couldn't hide it, maybe it was like a trophy one of those that is expected to be applauded and honored for life.

Before killing him, he wanted to look him in the eye, it was something that he always did religiously to all the prisoners without knowing why.

Ros?

Yes, it's me.

And are you Joan?

Yes, the same one who lent you the shoes for your first communion.

You remember that day?

Yes, it was the last time I laughed and felt like a child.

And what are you doing here Joan?

Play war.

And you Ros?

Pray to save my life.

Can you help me Joan?

Your men have killed my parents, they have taken what I loved most. I am a child like you who does not want to stop laughing and dreaming.

You can help me and by the way you help yourself.

What do you mean?

Let's both escape.

Don't think about it Joan.

I beg you.

But I also lost my parents to the subversion and I want to avenge their deaths.

But I am also a victim of the armed confrontation Joan, I am not guilty of the death of yours.

My life is in your hands.

Help me, Joan, let's escape.

Joan looked around as if searching for an answer.

You kill him or I kill him, the man with the gun shouted.

No, I'll kill him, Joan told him.

You're not serious, are you?

Johan didn't answer; he carried the rifle to his chest; a shot rang out and then another; the man with the gun smiled at him and fired several shots into the air as a sign of joy.

He's already dead, he's on his way to hell at this hour, Joan told him.

Way to go, way to go.

Do I throw it in the river? Yes, for the piranhas to swallow that son of a bitch.

Joan reached over and untied it.

Open your eyes, you are not dead.

I'm not dead?

Why did you do this?

For the shoes you gave me for my first communion.

Thank you little friend, God take care of you.

You too.

Nothing deep, when you get to the shore do not take the roads, they are full of bankruptcy mines.

When Ros reached the shore he heard two shots, looked back and saw Joan fall horizontally into the water. Behind him was the man with the smoking gun still screaming, that traitors were going straight to hell.

Ros felt guilt for his death, but armed himself with other thoughts to make his journey to the place of silences easier. On the other side of the river were the guerrillas; men the color of the jungle, some barefoot, bony, and full of malaria. There were children like him, perhaps with the same story or worse, but that was his country full of blood, full of thistles and dreams to achieve. There was Reis, one of the oldest commanders leading the oldest organization on the continent; He hugged him and cried with him his mourning.

Reis invited him to avenge the death of his parents, but he told him that he was just a child, that he wanted to grow up and study and deal with his own pain, not with violence but in a spiritual way.

Spiritual? Reis replied.

Is there another way to change the feeling of loss with prayers?

Your parents will not forgive you for forgiving the murderers with prayers, while they continue mourning the roads with more blood.

And did you lose yours?

Yes, that's why I'm here.

For how long?

Until the last of them dies.

I thought that the revolution was a social act and not an act of hatred.

Both, my little grasshopper. We humans, sometimes need emotional reasons to do what we would not do without them, to kill someone you have to hate them, and to want to change the world we have to feel love for life, and for those who cannot do anything to change it for fear or omission.

I do not understand his red philosophy, I hope when he grows up he will understand it.

He will undoubtedly understand it, even though it doesn't take me a thousand years to understand what he had to do.

Do you feel good about what you do?

Yes, but I'll feel better when it's all over.

What?

Revenge or revolution?

Both.

Can I ask you something?

Sure, it is part of the democracy we want to build.

Who killed your parents?

The same ones who killed yours.

May I know how?

His gaze changed and a few tears came out of his eyes, which he wiped away with the back of his left hand. Then he sat on a mound of grass as he took from his wallet a letter gnawed at by the years

This letter was written by my father to my mother three days before he was murdered.

I was three years old at the time.

"My dear Yedra, I am fleeing from death day and night; I have fallen and risen, my feet are tired and my heart is weak. I think of you and my little Reis; I assume I am a condor with large wings that does not want to stop flying until it is free and to meet you again if I get out alive. I hear shots behind my back but in an act of magic I escape without knowing how.

How long?

I don't know, but if something happens in the mist of time I will take care of them; There I will build a large nest for when the owners of power knock on their doors they will not find them, there we will dream until the night passes and they can return home. I hope my death is not one more; They will not need big shoes to follow the route to the sun if my executioners take refuge there.

My beloved Reis, I never thought that this would touch me for thinking differently, but the history of men cannot be changed when there is an open book where we record our lives, also our deaths. When you become a man you will understand that it is difficult to close your eyes and cover your ears, when there is a judge in front of you who wants to condemn you because he thinks he is the owner of the law and of men.

I did not choose to be a fugitive, I only dreamed of leaving the door of dreams open but this will cost me my life.

A big kiss for both of us.

I love you".

Reis

And how did they kill him?

Tortured

And your mother?

She died of moral pain at six months.

And how did you become a partisan?

I looked for them when I was your age.

Was your father an insurgent?

No, he was a communal leader

My name is Reis.

And yours?

Ros.

You stay?

No, not yet.

Where are you going?

To the great capital.

With whom?

I have one uncle left.

Best of luck my little grasshopper, you are welcome anytime.

Thanks.

Goodbye and remember that we are one family here.

When the commander's men put him on a backpacking bus, he felt his roots linger with crickets and birdsong. He cried out the farewell to his environment and now more than ever the death of his parents. During the trip, the commander's last words were rolling in his head: "we are one family".

His uncle had been missing for six months when he participated in International Labor Day. He wandered the streets and ate at garbage cans. He befriended hunger and loneliness as well, but he never tried drugs. He lived as a recycler and there he met his future wife Nara. Soon he became president of the union of the guild but that same overturned him to exile. The far right accused him of being a communist and the attacks on him and his family did not stop. There was no protection from state agencies and nowhere to hide.

The first attempt on his life occurred the day he was negotiating a list of labor demands.

It was a miracle to be alive. A high-explosive bomb was remotely activated in the building where thirteen people died and one got seriously injured. Three months after his recovery, another attack was immediate. An armed man intercepted him at a traffic light, but he counted on the good luck that the gun jammed and he was able to escape unscathed.

Ros never thought that those above would push him to war, he also believed that change would be achieved through democratic means; but the spaces were completely closed and one day he remembered the words of the commander: "here we are a family"; So he packed his suitcases and went into the mountains to confront the militaristic and paramilitary wave, against any expression that restricted the rights of workers and the people in general.

The government had shut down the left-wing newspapers, arguing that they were destabilizing the country; the public universities had been closed by decree, because it said that from there the rebellion against the democratic government was brewing. The trade unionists were assassinated daily, and the peasants exiled by the paramilitary gang were supported by the army and the government.

His arrival was a party with strong corn "chichi", made with some spit according to the tradition of good drinkers, and some other shots into the air.

Reis was happy, he knew what this union leader represented for the guerrilla organization. His training and discipline made him worthy of military promotions and he soon gave the results expected by Reis. Guerrilla warfare was the spiral of their successes against the enemy. Attacking and retreating in enveloping circles left the enemy at a disadvantage. The prisoners of war did not wait and Ros became known as a good political negotiator, to the point of reaching the central command vertically. In less than a year he created a political movement of national convergence, but the extreme right assassinated almost four thousand leaders in the streets and sidewalks. The hope of achieving change through democratic means was an utopia. The war became general and knocked on the doors of all the inhabitants.

The people did not have time to think, to dream in those magical worlds where you navigate without thinking about the flash of a rifle, or avoid the pain of the pins burning your skin, it only mattered to know that you lived today so tomorrow you die.

Here, at the slightest carelessness, the passerby could be killed by a rifle blast; the peasant for a mine bankruptcy leg; fighters lose their lives in the blink of an eye.

Ros became the leader of the insurgency the day Reis died. For three days fierce fighting was fought in the center of the country; the machine-gunning by the government forces pushed back the rear of the insurgency until they were cornered on the Péndame river. Lieutenant Leguis landed hundreds of men, three kilometers behind where Reis was, and others as much ahead a kilometer. The helicopters began to make a sweep from above, while the two groups advanced over the river, tightening their encirclement. Reis had a small group of thirty men, hungry and some of them wounded and without medicine. He alerted his troops, and gave orders to break the fence and reach the mouth of the river that communicated the thick part of the jungle. Ros was more than seven kilometers away, fighting a fight to the death also with a group of soldiers stationed on the highest hill overlooking the river. Ros quickly made it to the river and began attacking the group of men behind Reis from the rear. The fighting became more intense as Reis's men tried to reach the mouth of the river. A grenade exploded in the face of Marion, a partisan who had been fighting for more than thirty years. The man screamed, then ran in no direction until he fell doubled over on the rocks.

Move forward!, companions, forward; revolution or death ! Reis yelled as he fired his rifle. There was no time to collect the dead, nor to mourn them.

I'm hurt Reis, I'm hurt. It was Sion, a fighter who had been fighting alongside Reis all his life and who had entered the movement when he had no other path of life other than this. He had a shot in the left leg, he crawled as best as he could and managed to get where he was.

Your leg is shit from the knee down, it's hanging by a thread.

Take the rest away, she told him amid shouts.

Reis took out his knife, cut it off, and bandaged it. A cry of pain crossed the mountains and then came a spasm of pain that embedded itself in all who heard its cry.

Stay there, buddy, we're going to get out of this, I promise you.

Leguis continued landing specialized support groups on the south eastern side, it was the only clearing that the rebels had to get out of the crossroads.

We have a helicopter in our heads that is vomiting lead at us, these sons of bitch want to fuck us, yelled Gemí, the youngest woman in the group.

Let's give it all in series, Reis told them. Everyone heard the roar and in the midst of it the dying voice of Zion screaming: we hit the son of a bitch, we hit him!

Reis was signaling to Dante, the soldier who armed with a thirty point would not let them advance. He looked everywhere and there with an enigmatic gaze was Ni, Reis's sentimental partner giving him the victory sign when he shot him she saw him fall horizontally to the ground.

One, two, three and more helicopters were dropping tons of bombs on the hill. It was as if the world was going to go up in flames. Behind a roar came others, and with them the hill collapsed, burying some of the combatants and soldiers. Some ran but were hit, first by explosive waves and then by rocks, dirt and mud. The river was dammed, and on the third day it washed away an abandoned hamlet in poverty, where Reis had been born forty-seven years ago.

Ros managed to evacuate the area with his men and save some of the inhabitants, mainly children and the elderly. The loss of human life was great and the environmental disaster was unprecedented in the history of the country. Leguis apologized for the military strategy used but no one brought him to justice.

Nara had not seen him again for seven years, he only kept a letter that he had written to him when his son Ros was one year old. She knew he was alive even though the media considered him dead. Many times he read his letter and there he could imagine the day to day of his life in the thick forest, and the anxiety to liberate his people from the tyrant who had subjected them.

"My dear Nara, today I hear the crickets sing and the frogs jump over the mud where we have to strain the water to drink; on the plastics that serve as tiles I hear the water running, and the cold creeping up on our bones. The night is dark and the sky is full of clouds full of water and lightning. I also feel the smell of our sweaty bodies and the breath of hunger eating our intestines. A year ago the planes bombed the camp, the ground was covered in flames and the birds did not fly because a rain of fire bombs burned their wings.

That night the sky turned red and the trees creaked, the grass turned to ashes and death threw a great party at midnight. Nicolás did not have time to pick up his Habanero tobacco, because at that moment we saw him fly through the trees and his cheerful smile lost in the din. He always said that death might be like a passage where there were many lights, and that one died when they ran out of fuel.

Araní was by his side, we never found his body, maybe the grass turned into ashes, like death when it takes over life. She is gone now, he is too, perhaps the two of them are now weaving the time of change so that the path of the struggle is shorter, and the liberation of our people is the toast of the party. Lina and Jacob were stationed behind the ravine, there they fought until a bomb burned their bones. The night before they had told us the dream of the white butterflies, who were going to liberate us from the cruel world of war. The butterflies were forming a large balloon and inside we were all holding hands. The land from above looked green, and in the sea paper boats carried people to a place where weapons were museums, and peace a common good of humanity. The hot air balloon went around the world and the world was as we had dreamed it. We looked into each other's eyes and in each of them we found other balloons that were returning to earth, because there were no more shots, peace had won the war, and war was nothing more than a word that nobody wanted to remember.

We returned to the place where they had begun to dream, but when we reached the land the white butterflies moved away; We began to float on a river where there were men dressed as military men who fired at us without respite. The sky was covered with planes that spewed fire, and they did not listen to us telling him, that we were men of peace, that we no longer wanted war, that he was a monster with a thousand heads that destroyed the dreams of humanity and pulverized innocent lives. But they did not stop, and that was when they climbed the ravine and the bombs ended their lives.

Do you believe in dreams? Jacob asked us, smoking his long habanero tobacco. Alan replied in the dark that dreams sometimes have bad premonitions.

Are we going to die in the ravine, Lina and I? Stop bullshitting, I replied.

Camilo and I from the opposite side of the ravine we faced the plane; the other companions crossed the river, and from the bushes set them on fire with lead. The plane kept dropping bombs and we even thought it was the end of the world. The flames began to engulf the trees, and men were now parachuting from the plane in different directions. I don't know how it happened or who hit the target, but now we saw it fall into the river. We did an enveloping operation and they soon fell as prisoners of war. We released them naked on the seventh day with a message of victory, and an invitation to government forces to join our fight.

My dear Nara, the path to travel is not the same as the path of dreams, but they are there crossing the bridge between the real and the imaginary world; they are like pendulums of time marking defeat or victory, joy or sadness. Here I stay until the roads meet dreams, and we can all fearlessly dream the same dream, and see the moon and the sun with the same eyes. Tell Ros that he is my seed, and that I hope when he is my age, will travel through the winds spreading the word freedom where spaces are closed; that beyond where the sun rises I am building libertarian dreams so that we sleep with the doors open, without fear of our dreams being assaulted.

Reis and many companions have died; my heart is sad, but I will continue on my way to the sun where the big door will open and store dreams of love and freedom.

Goodbye, my dear Nara ".

They did not realize how they grew, nor how they became an irregular army that now inflicted significant casualties on the army, and they were in a guerrilla war in the cities and in the countryside, where they had some cities under their control. But in her diary she noted that this time would come and it would be then that the ships of dreams of what Lina and Jacob dreamed would bring other dreams, not to leave the land and dream imaginary dreams, but to make them come true.

He and his men were at the outpost in the capital, right there where secret state agencies had dissolved the student committee and the unions, where they had been imprisoned and tortured to the point of fingernails and scars on their souls. They did not know exactly when they would achieve victory, but that did not depend on the dead placed on the two sides, it was a matter of a few more deserting the side of the government troops and continuing to join them.

Among the deserters was Aaron with a group of men, who in a combat slipped down the slope until they reached the other side of the river, where the insurgents were stationed and made the outposts at night to attack the enemy. The lieutenant cursed and swore on the demons to make them swallow their own shit when he got their hands on it.

Long live the revolution! Aaron yelled.

Long live! They all answered. Ros was happy, it was part of the fight report for his men and the moral discouragement for the enemy troop.

After a year Aaron became the lieutenant of Ros and the second man in command in the national leadership.

From the windows of the buildings eaten by the flames, men with white flags peeked out, while the rifles and the tanks with their thirty points fired their last cartridges. This was the day everyone had dreamed of, the day of final victory.

At the side of the street there were eyes that communicated joys, other claimants asked about the dead. The happiness of some was the song of pain between pins for others, the same when the skin melts by the sun, like the voices of the one who dies when they are wrapped in the sounds of the night. Large moons and suns, trees grown with hope in the heart of the combatant who savored victory, tears of pain and blood of those who lost it. The difference between pain and joy cannot be measured when crossing the bridge, when bodies are shipwrecked in the waters with their eyes looking at the sky, and others dance intoxicated by those who lose their lives crossing the bridge. This is what Nara thought, locked in her dark thoughts; she was afraid that he was one of those who crossed the bridge, or maybe he would travel through the waters with his eyes open saying goodbye to her.

There were other imaginaries where, lying on the dry grass with bloody hands, he asked for water, but the dead demanded life from him and left him without looking back. Also there was the hero riding on black horses clinging to his mane, and a multitude that revered him to the unspeakable, others that hated him.

She took her son and wanted to know if his imaginaries had life, or perhaps they were part of the dreams that he had stored up for such a long wait. He read his letter one last time and found the breath to demystify his long-standing fears. The street was crowded with the dead and others ran to the main square. He looked among the dead, did not find it. Then she felt her heart beat faster and she imagined him with his long beard and sun-tanned hair. Snipers were standing between the windows of the buildings. He could see them with their big rifles pointing at the running people. They were dressed in black with government insignia. It was the counter revolution armed and paid for by those who did not resign themselves to losing power.

"Paramilitaries, sons of bitch", she thought after crossing the street called "the route of death", it was called like that because dozens of people who had tried to escape had died there, the day the army repressed the first demonstration in against the old dictator.

She heard a thud; then she saw how the earth opened up and ate the large ceiba tree in the park where she used to take her son to raise balloons. She took refuge in the rubble of a building with her son, and it was when she saw a group of people who were also taking refuge in the adjoining building fly in flames through the air. The plane kept strafing and dropping bombs in different directions, until the resistance men shot it down.

Where can I run away? There was the stadium, a hundred meters from there where she also used to go with Aaron to watch his favorite soccer team. The men in the buildings kept shooting but they kept running. A shot struck her leg, she fell, she got up.

Are you hurt mommy?

Yes, son, yes.

You can walk?
I think so, help me.
Where we go?
To the stadium.
As she crossed the street, two shots exploded Nara's other leg.
Run away son, run away!
I can't leave you mother.
It does not matter, you are the seed that will grow and bring water for the green grass to grow, and for others to dream of the peace that those who do not dream need so much.
Yes, but I can't leave you.
When Ros couldn't lift her, he bandaged her sweater on both legs, and settled into a fetal position next to his mother.
Mommy, we are in the midst of the dead; In the buildings there are snipers, they have eyes of hatred and thirst for blood, he began by saying. The pendulum between life and death has marked the opposite direction to our wills: to live in harmony with our fellow human beings. Last night when we were watching the death of the child who crossed the street when I stepped on a bomb, I fell asleep. There in that dream was my father. He had a large beard and a green beret with a red star in the center. He approached, lifted me in his arms and said: "There are roads that are full of lives, they are white and on the sides there are dreams that walk with other dreams hand in hand. They are like angels from another world, they laugh and also cry when some road dies. On those roads there are flags, some of them are broken but they flutter with the wind, others the flames consume them while we look at them as if they were not ours, out of fear or omission.

And what are the other paths? I asked him as I walked with him hand in hand on those white roads.

They are the ways of death.

And don't those roads have white dreams to take care of you?

No, they killed them before they were roads, son.

Why?

We all live in the world but not all of us want peace.

Peace is a white bird that flies, it is like a spirit that is within us reaping the wheat of the kiss, of the embrace, of the encounter of dreams of life, even if we are black, white, Indian or mixed.

And if you love peace, why are you in war?

It is a way of achieving it when the other paths end, when they deny us the right to expression and equality, she concluded by telling him.

Now in the midst of everything he remembered what his father told him in one of his letters, if I die before seeing the wheat give the seed of my struggle, and you and your mother survive, I will be on the white path of dreams caring for you with a sun in my head. That will be the light that will lead them to pick up the steps that I walked, the joy that I lived and the nostalgia that I felt when having them far from me. Do not mourn my death, it will be the pendulum for others to continue in the search for permanent happiness.

And do you think son, that we manage to be the seed that your father says, when there are hundreds of snipers shooting us to kill?

Yes, mother, we will be seeds; so let's die today.

They won't be seeds, a voice behind them yelled.

Are you going to kill us?

Yes, because you are communist seeds.

And who are you? The boy asked him.

The black road that will lead you to death.

Let us live, Nara told him.

Kill me if you want, but let him live.

When the man drew the revolver, the two understood that the journey to death was unappealable, but that they would be seeds that would grow among the ashes of the dead to be somewhere arming Ros's dreams.

There were thirteen shots that came in dry one after another. They were dead, but he wanted to keep shooting at them; He had no more bullets, so he yelled at someone else to shoot them from there. It was a big weapon, because the bodies were scattered between the lamp posts and the stadium.

A kilometer from there, Ros stood in the main square with his rifle raised. His voice was there traveling with the wind, his words were doves that soared through the sky, and then nested in the hearts of the spectators.

"This victory is not mine, I am just a pawn of the revolution who has made a dream so that we all dream the same dream, and we fly in doves through the air without fear of losing our wings. We will be a seed and a tree; we will be new water where life will grow; We will be roads where muleteers will walk without fear of thorns. Those who are not here from somewhere in the universe look at us, they are warming our feet in the long march through life, they are with their eyes open giving us the light to continue step by step the dream of Bolívar, Che, Martí, and of all those who could not see the plowed road.

Here we will build the new man from the ruins left by the war, but first we will plant olive trees in the place of the unknown soldier, the fallen partisans, and all those who the armed conflict took their lives from. When I was a child I never thought I would be a combatant, I never imagined seeing my brothers die on the battlefront; but sometimes what we neither want nor desire, others are there at the point of shrapnel, pushing us to war, breaking our destinies.

Let me tell you I hate war, it has taken away my dreams as a child, now I will have to deal with ghosts and goblins in my bed. I hope that in your windows the white bird of peace accompanies you, and that on the roads that we still have to go, someone will give us espadrilles.

Let me also tell you that at night I have cried and I have even thought that our God is not benevolent with our sufferings; do not ask me why, but reasons are not lacking. I only know that this revolution belongs to us and that we are barely beginning to fight for it. I want all of us to embrace the meeting and forgive each other for the damage caused ".

He walked through the crowd looking for the warm embrace of Nara and her little Ros but did not find them; he yelled their name, asked about them but no one gave him reason. Among the buildings eaten by ashes a shot struck his chest. The light in his eyes was slowly lost and an icy cold took over his body. He saw them on the white road with their hands outstretched trying to reach hers; On the shore there were other hands that were saying goodbye to him with red flowers, and on the other side of a river a large sign that read: "Goodbye, Commander Ros." He heard his words of farewell as if they came from a dark pitcher, but he could no longer decipher them. He went along a bridle path where there were giant trees, and on the trees men who built dreams of peace for which he had fought. He was happy to see them, because he considered them dreams and seeds of his revolution.

The dreamer, the man who had built bunches of dreams, was dead; There were no miracles to resuscitate him, not something magical either, he had left without returning but he was still present in the heart of the town.

Who the fuck killed him?

Who?

The cry of one and the other grew, and each one searched among them for the murderer. Three shots rang out and another man fell from the top of the building. Behind was Aaron with his rifle still sparkling and his eyes full of hatred.

The general is dead, the son of a bitch is dead! Aaron yelled from the balcony with panache.

The crowd ran and after a short time no one gave an account of the general's body.

Aaron was still enveloped in gray smoke that was still coming out of the building; He seemed a being that came from beyond to avenge the death of the man who one day took a rifle, and without espadrilles walked with a lot of dreams that he dreamed of until the end of his life.

The new leader of the mass, of the people, was there at the side of the revolution, singing victory with his rifle raised high, and with his calm but courageous voice he urged them to close the gap that divides the rich and the poor, the hunger of some, and the abundance of others.

"They will ask me why I am here next to you and not next to the government, why have I taken up arms against them; You have the reason when the suffering of living creeps into our bodies and in our dreams, and in every corner we see our children asking for bread, the elderly dying of hunger and cold in the streets. In terms of warfare, they have used weapons against the people themselves, and we are the people who plow the land and breathe in the burnt oil from the factories.

The paramilitaries have committed all kinds of genocides in complicity with the military, and have made torture official as a way of obtaining confessions and imprisoning those who think differently from the regime.

Long live the revolution! Long live the revolution!

Some applauded their new leader, others mourned the fallen idol, it was a mixture of mixed feelings where each one released their hatreds, also their fears.

Aní had her heart exalted with emotion and her feelings sailed above her head. When he walked towards her she did not seem to be walking, it seemed that she was flying on white butterflies and that time released that long-awaited wait. She saw him beautiful, and even thought it was an angel who came from another world to free his people from the ignominy and slavery of the ruler.

Here she was with her open arms waiting for him where everyone is not, and if they are, they do not know who they are, because the war might have eaten their memory.

Tears, hugs and kisses spread to everyone in the main square; some took out white handkerchiefs, others celebrated with rifle shots in the air.

Aní, where is our son?

Where is Aaron?

Where?

She looked at him with infinite sadness and he immediately understood his absence.

Oh God, it was the greatest thing we both had. Is it true?

This was said with a voice broken by crying and with a trembling in his body that he could not contain. It was our seed, our dream of love, she answered him.

Many things have happened since my departure, and in this long wait there have been dreams, but we never dreamed of the loss of our Aaron

Yes, that is the consequence of the war.

Damn war, he concluded.

They had other words to say to each other, perhaps navigating other imaginary worlds where they had never dreamed, but they flew away wrapped in twisted iron, and in a smoke screen that covered the entire city when the bomb exploded.

The snipers began firing in close fire from the other buildings, while Lieutenant Leguis with a regiment of men was present at the scene. A bomb was thrown at the church where the resistance was facing and where some civilians were taking refuge. Some of the survivors went up in flames within them the priest, the others were buried in the rubble.

The counter revolution had arrived; the country was at war again; The fighting fronts spread throughout the country and each one of them was creating other structures of political and military power, while the forces of order made alliances with far-right groups, mainly with the paramilitaries, who were in charge of creating terror. the civilian population with their barbaric acts. Each one of the sides took position and again men began to float in the rivers, and the ghosts of bad dreams sneaked through the cracks of the houses.

Lieutenant Leguis rose to a seven-star general overnight, and military and ideological leaders emerged from the insurgency as great as Reis, Ros, and Aarón.

Each man became an instrument of war, where the dreams of Ros, Reis, Aaron and all those who died, were now seeds of a soil fertilized with dreams that one day hoped to make them come true.

General Leguis created scaffolding on his own feet to walk as fast as time behind communist seeds.

Nobody but them, those faced in that war where the joy of some was the death of the other, those who were in the center had to take sides on one of the sides, because whoever had a weapon had the power, and whoever that did not have it, he was called to dig his own grave.

On a corner of the town's main street, someone read: "Birds no longer fly because they don't have wings; the rifles are not silent because the last combatant has not fallen ".